Belly
of the
Whale

Belly
of the
Whale

Sonia Amer

PARTRIDGE

To order additional copies of this book, contact
Toll Free 800 101 2657 (Singapore)
Toll Free 1 800 81 7340 (Malaysia)
orders.singapore@partridgepublishing.com

www.partridgepublishing.com/singapore

Contents

Foreword vii

Introduction ix

Part One 1

Part Two 10

Part Three 14

Part Four 18

Part Five 23

Part Six 28

Part Seven 32

Part Eight 36

Part Nine 40

Part Ten 44

Part Eleven 49

Part Twelve, the Finale 57

About the Translator 63

Foreword

"Belly of the Whale" and Dreams of Futile Salvation
Feras Haj Mohamed / Palestine

I HAVE STARTED READING "BELLY OF the Whale" by the Lebanese writer Sonia Amer with the sensibility of a critic in mind. Soon enough, I was taken away from my critical sense by the splendor of the text and led into a world of pure aesthetic pleasure. The more I tried to subjugate the reading to my critical consciousness, the more it evaded me; I found myself ensnarled into the depth of the novel with its twists and turns. It felt like I was trying to walk on barbed wire in a field full of hidden explosives without ever losing my critical consciousness. I have tried over and over again, and every time the striking and fresh architecture of this intense novel overcame my criticism.

The novel falls into a few pages of unfussy build but it is not to be judged simply by that. It is lavish in portraying many human lives and several political, social, philosophical and existential ideas. Moreover, the writer has rebelliously left linguistic gaps in the structure so that you, the reader, could participate in making your own novel. You might find yourself embodied in one of the characters who have tussled for so long with existential concepts and searched tirelessly for salvation by all means, even if death itself was the salvation. The line **"I face death by expiring in my passion perhaps someday I would die as I always wished"** seems to sum up the theme of the novel.

Belly of the Whale is a novel that breaths freshness and comes with a unique taste. Its bitterness is enough to make you delve deeply into yourself and to bring you face to face with your reality. The ideas it hosts encourage you to reconsider your actions in life. Thus, you end up either as one of the thousand deluded searchers for deceptive happiness or as someone who crystalizes life around a single solid and supreme idea that leads towards enlightenment so that you can be your own guide and the savior of your own soul. The salvation sought here is a complete human salvation that does not lead to a disastrous death in case you had chosen to continue living in vicious circles that lead you nowhere. Bottom line, life, as the novel sees it, is not an absurd or lascivious journey but rather a decision that you and me do take by our free will.

Introduction

ONCE UPON A TIME, DEEP into the ocean, there was a fable named "Belly of the Whale" that was big enough for a thousand people to live in; half of them were men and the other half women. Everyone in Belly of the Whale had to be in disguise and they had to be married couples. There were conditions for their arrival as well: each spouse had to arrive alone, wearing new clothes that the other had never seen before so that it was impossible for them to recognize their partners. With everyone on board of Belly of the Whale, the party began and a journey of unconditional, unlimited enjoyment started. No one would ever see the other again, or even get to know them during the party. They were not even allowed to speak in the true tone of their voices so that they might not be identified by their partners. It was dangerous to be revealed through one's voice and once a recognized by his/her partner through voice, the other partner had to throw the recognized one into the sea. That was the rule of the game. Men, as well as women, tried to disguise in all possible manners: to fake their movements, their laughs, and even their favorite foods and drinks; it was extremely dangerous to be revealed; the end was clear and predetermined and mistakes were intolerable.

Everything went just fine and everyone wished to spend the rest of their lives in Belly of the Whale and never to leave it. A few hours later, women started to feel bored, and men felt sleepy; all of them wanted to go back home, to sleep and maybe to make love. But they were not entitled to go out; their salvation relied only on staying disguised endlessly since in Belly of the Whale time did not pass and people did not get old nor died. What could they do? Was there no way out? Each woman began to think on her own, some of them decided to just enjoy the ride spontaneously and start to get to know others on board, not bothering about the rules of the game. The only thing they cared about was changing the tone of their voices, and their habits; some of the women succeeded to do so, and some excelled; how could not they succeed when it was the only chance to change their boring lives?

Men, on the other hand, were very happy because it was time to change their spouses, and in so doing, they were doing the resourcefully disguised women a favor. Many fell in love, and several thanked God for sending them to Belly of the Whale, not bothering about the things or the people they had left behind on earth where, eventually, their children would grow up, their money would not last forever and their own lives would come to an end; nothing was worthy of regret or sorrow. All on board got acquainted to one another using their fake names and the fake identities they impersonated. Months and years went by as the invaders of Belly of the Whale felt happy and elated; there were no children to be born and raised to go to school, no one would have to make a living in order to get married, no one would ever age or die; life was one non-stop, non-ending party inside Belly of the Whale. One day, one of the men could identify his real wife. Inspired by his infatuation with her, he could recognize the scent of her body, which he had used to describe as the smell of amber. Fearing for her life, the poor husband never mentioned that he recognized her true identity because she would be thrown into the sea for not taking great pains to disguise properly. So, he suppressed his yearning for her and sufficed himself with watching her moving freely and having fun.

Many years went by and none of them ever felt tired or sick; they were all eager for freedom and love; no one got thrown into the sea since they all managed to do a good job disguising. Soon enough, things suddenly changed; boredom started to leak into their souls; they resisted fatigue, disease, and drowsiness and, above all, their longing for their previous lives on land. They did not know how to overcome boredom, how could they overcome it when some of them loved or hated one another and problems started to arise as if they had never gotten into Belly of the Whale? When they were fed up with the illusion of eternity, they all decided to commit suicide, and off they jumped into the sea; some of those who miraculously survived met one another by accident on land.

Part One

H ALA THANKED GOD: THANK YOU God, I have been set free finally, I have waited so long until I almost doubted the miracle could ever happen. When I joined this bizarre secret Association, I thought it was just a game; I never imagined that God had put it my way as a means for my salvation. Hala was thirty, and married, married against her will despite the fact that she was the one who forced herself into marrying that famous wealthy man. Like her name connotes, Hala[1] was sweet; she was blond, blue eyed and willowy like a woman from French origins. She gave birth to a girl and a boy only because her (prestige)[2] would not allow her to have more children and spoil her figure; she would not allow herself to go under the knife of a plastic surgeon unless it is something trivial like a lipoid suction or a tightening of a floppy tummy. Despite the strict diet she followed during pregnancy, she gained incredible weight, almost thirty kilos because of the so-called gestational diabetes which made her to feel hungry all the time and caused water retention, or what doctors called albumin. But thank God, this condition did not affect her babies who were born healthy and beautiful. Her son Adam weighted five kilos at birth and doctors feared that he might be diabetic but he was not. Hala insisted that her beauty was a hundred percent natural;

---

[1]   The word Hala in Arabic means either something sweet, a beautiful woman, or jewelry.

[2]   Emphasis by writer

her angelic face needed no makeup. She got married when she was twenty two, a fresh graduate at the department of psychology in the prestigious university, with honors. Despite her stunning beauty, Hala was a very sensitive and ambitious person and she loved money and fame. She was crowned Miss Beauty of the beach for 2008 and was a candidate for Miss Lebanon but withdrew her candidacy on the last moment on the advice of her wealthy fiancé and her mother. Her mother reminded her of Suzanne Tamim[3], another beauty icon, and how her life ended sadly. Hala feared that she might end up like her if she became a target for fashion agencies; she was freighted by the huge pressures that come along with fame, and did not want to become a commodity in the hands of beauty vendors.

Hala first met her husband in a party during her first year in the university; she was playing the role of Isis in a play named after the goddess of love. Prestigious, famous on the local and global levels, and wealthy, he was a member of the university board of directors who owned 60 percent of its shares. This made him the largest financer of the university with its political affiliations which served his own purposes. That was a clever attitude, and maybe someday his work necessitated his participation in the political arena, anything could happen.

Hala came from a modest family and therefore studying in such a prestigious university was no coincidence or out of pure luck. It came as a result of a great sacrifice from Mona, Hala's mother, who sold the land she inherited from her mother. Mona had no siblings to split the inheritance with and the piece of land she inherited was situated in a beautiful and wealthy neighborhood so the price she got for it was so high that it actually saved Hala and her three younger sisters. Hala's parents were keen on having a son; they tried hard but at no avail. The result of their feverish attempts to get a baby boy was a family of four

---

3   Suzanne Tamim was a Lebanese singer who rose to fame in the Arab world after winning the top prize in the popular Studio El Fan television show in 1996. She was murdered brutally in Dubai in July 2008.

girls with the mother a retired teacher and the father a postman in the ministry of communications struggling all month to make ends meet; the ministry never did justice to postmen.

With Hala married to a wealthy man, her sisters' chances to study in prestigious universities improved. Their brother in law was desperate to help and was always wont on pleasing Adam's mother and his in laws. No matter how hard Hala tried to keep herself busy, she always felt there was something missing. She did not have a job, and she definitely did not need one; she spent her time in social engagements, parties, sponsorship of orphanages and the elderly and in the distribution of charities to the needy. All these activities, however, did not consume eight hours' worth of daily work, not even in one of her husband's companies. To fill up the void in her days, she maximized her weekly sports program which included aerobics, jogging, running, and swimming. Then she took it a step further with the practice of yoga and long hours of meditation and spiritual communication until she fulfilled an extremely advanced level in these practices got acquainted to the wonderful group of the Association that led her into what they call the eternal paradise: Belly of the Whale.

Hala had always wanted to contact that handsome young man. She recalled the day she got acquainted with him; he was then president of a Scouts team affiliated with a political party that supported her university. He frequently visited the university to hold festivals and participate in plays in which Hala always played the heroine. She was a clever actress, especially when it came to the roles of romantic, beautiful girls which caused her many problems with other girls who could not compete with her neither in beauty nor in cleverness. Jealousy and nothing other than jealousy was what they felt for her. Hala smiled to herself triumphantly and recalled the words of her best friends, words that she will never forget: "had you been less beautiful Hala, my life would have been much better!" That young man, however, was so handsome he could compete with her in beauty; he belonged to the same laboring social class like her. Nevertheless, they were different in a significant way: while she was ambitious and full of aspirations, he held tightly to his principles. And then Mr. Lucky came her way, Mister Maher, Sorbonne graduate, French cultured and director of a prestigious bank who. Due to a final donation to the university which exceeded half a million dollars, he became Chairman of the Board of Directors.

Preparations for the marriage did not last for long, within three months everything was ready: a luxurious apartment in a wealthy neighborhood, Italian furniture, Iranian carpets, and world-famous paintings. She would never have accepted less than an Yves Saint Laurent wedding gown and an Audi, her favorite car with new features that matched her ever changing temperament. She thought about having the wedding party in Miami Beach, as it was the trend to do those days, but sufficed herself with Venice to save some money to help her sisters register in prestigious universities. Hala was never a selfish person; she always shared her happiness with others. Even the list of guests and the invitation cards were made out of papyrus to remind her of her pharaonic characteristics and her love of that civilization. The cards were wrapped in velvet and Chinese silk, with a gold coin engraved with the names of the bride and groom as a token of appreciation and paying back for those who gave them wedding presents.

Hala did not deny spending happy days with Maher, very happy days actually, roaming the cities of world: Rome, Paris, New York and other cities. She saved Australia for winter and was preparing herself to enjoy its sunny weather had it not been to the sudden Whale journey which turned her world upside down.

Every time Hala visited a new country, she saw herself as a totally new person, a person she hardly knew. She would not take her children Adam and Tamara along in those trips; they had their own life style as children and would not be able to understand or hand the weird unstable life she lived.

That was why they spent most of their time with their loving grandmother who devoted herself completely to them after resigning from her teaching job because of excruciating back pain. She had always served her family single-handedly; maids were not available back them as they were today. With Adam and Tamara around, Mona almost established a semi-permanent residence at her daughter's apartment. Her marital obligations towards her husband became almost nonexistent due to old age, or maybe due to the huge frustrations that kept accumulating into the kind hearted Ryad, Hala's father, fossilizing inside him and preventing him to lead a normal married life.

Thank God; mother agreed to live with my children for good. I will be having this no return experience in the Belly of the Whale, the journey I insist on making more than anything else, more than ever. I was astounded when I surprised Manoush[4], my mother, with my blessed decision, I expected her to be surprised, to shout and threaten but the reaction I got from her was surprisingly unusual. She did not show any fear nor refusal nor worry; she looked quiet and content as if God was trying her faith with a calamity that she willingly accepted. Mona's words of acceptance astonished Hala: "You could have chosen a far more reckless path, my dear daughter, and I thank God that your search for bliss is not riddled with harm. I am happy and content for you. It is your destiny and God's choice for you; God has chosen you for a mission that we do not understand. You have gone so far into the world of meditation and spirituality with highly ranked people; so go dear daughter and God will always chose what is best for you".

What is the problem? Why have we got that far? How did we come to that crazy agreement? How did we come to participate in this risky venture? Our agreement to do so was a disguised bargain to escape from one another, was not that a hideous escape? I am thrilled about the Belly of the Whale, it is something never seen by a human eye or heard by a human ear, something no mortal had ever tried! "Paradise on earth" was the term the Chairman of the Association used to describe it; he assured us it was a paradise.

"Please be careful, I want to change everything about my hair: the color, the cut and the way it is done. I am attending is a Masquerade, as

---

4   Manoush" is a nick name for Mona

you know, but it is totally different from other parties. I do not want to be recognized, got what I mean? Nobody should be able to recognize who I am, even Maher." Hala said to the hairdresser.

"Don't worry Madame, and let me help you in my own way, I got your point, you want to surprise him like usual so that he can be more proud of you than ever. Why do you look so worried? This is so unlike you; it is not the first time you hold a party, even if it was a mascaraed? Trust me Madame, would you like a cup of coffee?" The stylist said.

Sandra was more than a hairstylist to Hala; she was her friend and confidant to whom she disclosed ten percent of her secrets, which was a good percentage considering Hala's cautious nature. Despite her extreme simplicity, Hala often felt lonely; she felt unbearably isolated especially when she was more engaged into social activity. The more engaged with others she got, the more strangled she felt. Social engagement was never a relief; it was a barrier, a rope around her neck that brought her nothing but a feeling of suffocation.

Sandra was a kindhearted and seasoned women whose experience was totally different from Hala's and it was that difference that attracted Hala towards the disguised friendship she and Sandra developed. Sandra's craftsmanship taught her to respect borders between herself and her clients; she would never trespass these borders with Hala; she adopted a policy of seeing and listening but never speaking. The short, stout, short-haired woman with honey colored eyes in her fifties goes on telling her story.

Sandra: Yes Madame; my daughter is a person with special needs.

Hala: But you never told me this before! How could you get her married? And I have seen her two babies and they look fine, how could that be so?

Sandra: Madame, women with special need have the same motherly instinct like us normal people. And mind you, my daughter was not born with special needs; her disability came as a result of the violence she suffered at the hands of her mother in law.

Hala: What? So you are not married? You never told me this!

Sandra: I was married Madame but I ran away from my husband's house and it took me ages to get back my daughter and when I did, she was disabled of violence.

Hala: So your other two girls came from your second marriage?

Sandra: Yes my friend; I got married again to a wealthy man but he wasted his money on women and gambling and, as you see, I am the one who supports the whole family. Thank God for everything.

Hala: Please go on, tell me about the big-hearted man who loved your daughter Soha despite her condition and married her.

Sandra: Don't get that wrong Madame! He too is mentally challanged but his family had promised that they will support him and take care of the children.

Hala: There is no power or might but Allah's[5]; go on Sandra; you keep surprising me.

Sandra: Unfortunately, his family did not keep their promise and now they want a divorce. So, my daughter and her two sons came to live with me and I am looking for a bigger house. I talked to a well-known lawyer to help her get alimony from her husband.

Hala gets lost in thoughts after hearing Soha's story. What type of person am I to complain after all what I have heard from Sandra? Oh my God! How evil and selfish I feel! I live in another world; I have to get back to the real world and help poor Sandra and Soha.

Hala: how long would it take you to finish this unusual hairdo, Sandra?

Hala was restless in her chair; she thought of the things she had to do before it goy dark. I need to spend some time with Tamara and Adam; I am not worried about them because Manoush will always be with them, but still my heart is broken and I cannot get over my maternal instinct. My trip might get long, who knows?"

Sandra: Madame, why don't you just cancel your party; you don't look well; your distracted looks worry me.

---

[5]   This is an expression or supplications that Muslims say when overwhelmed by a strange or a hard situation.

How can I go back on my word after the Association trusted me? I am extremely excited about this venture; I have to go on. Come on Hala! Come on! You have never been a coward.

I still cannot believe that Maher had accepted that crazy decision of mine. It is actually weird that he was more enthusiastic than me about starting this weird journey despite being aware of all the risks it involves. I have never really known that remarkable man; he is a mixture of perfection, genius and intelligence and I cannot even compete with him; he is such a unique person.

Waseem! How did I forget Waseem? I have to talk to him before I leave, just to say goodbye and to hear his voice one last time. Nobody knows how things will end up and maybe I will never come back again. I will not regret this courageous decision; we will have a happy ending, definitely. And I trust my Association and the Chairman.

Why am I so mad at him? Because he works all the time? Travels a lot? Because his is so handsome and attracts female attention? Is it because he is smart and perfect? I cannot find any fault in Maher. Is that why I am bored? My life is totally worry- free! I have no problem what so ever, could this be the reason? Maher is my husband, the father of my children and I love him. Why then the need for a new life? Why the feeling of insufficiency? What exactly I am looking for? My life is not lacking in feelings; I don't need more love or affection or sympathy. I don't deny that I admire his plumpness and his dark brown hair, striking features which lead the foreigners we meet in our travels to believe he is a Turk. I still remember his soft hands and expensive perfume; that was what attracted me to him in the first place on the day he handed me the best actress prize for my role in The Lady. I still remember how amazed he was with the way I performed the role of my beloved Lady Diana. He even envied Waseem for playing the role of Dody Elfayed and wished he was in his place. That sense of humor was always one of his characteristics ever since we accidently met. We talked about the love of Diana and Dody that remained in the dark and never saw daylight. The conversation then went on to discuss Prince Williams and Kate's wedding and how Lady Diana blessed their marriage, ordering rain not to fall in order not to spoil the occasion. That was a message from the loving mother to her oldest son on his wedding day; she blessed the marriage and was there for him all the time.

"Will you give me the pleasure to dance with you my Lady?"

"Of course, Sir. I'm honored," the disguised Hala answered, intoxicated with the prospect of utter liberty she had just started to enjoy in the eternal paradise. She started to dance, doing her best to change her usual style; she had to remind herself that Maher was there among the other guests and he might try to fool her and pretend he was someone else. Hala! Don't bother about these gloomy thoughts! Maher is just like you; he only wants to experience a new life, just for the sake of comparing the new and the old life styles.

"Which dance do you prefer my lady? Samba or Salsa or Tango or oriental dance? Just wish and your wish is my command; you are my guest tonight", said the amazing masked man.

The dance went great; as harmonious, smooth and full of love and simplicity as never before.

"Are you tired my Lady? Shall we rest for a while and have a drink?", asked the masked man.

Hala, now disguised as Laila, feels extremely happy to be asked to sit down; she had never in her life danced for such a long time. When a waiter asked them what to drink, Laila almost spontaneously ordered "orange juice" but she backed down immediately. Orange juice is her favorite drink but such an answer might reveal her identity since Maher knew that. If she ordered pineapple juice, which Maher knew she disliked, she might reveal her identity in the same manner. Maher would expect her to play such a trick by ordering the drink that disgusted her, though it was a good fat-burner; he knew she preferred pineapple as a fruit not as a juice. She ends up asking the waiter for apple juice.

Part Two

THE HANDSOME YOUNG MAN WHO danced with Laila had a very strange story. He was a playwright and a theatre director and he was the one who suggested the idea of eternity. He was a founding member in the Eternity Association which brought everyone to the Belly of the Whale and he had exerted great efforts to carry out the idea. Having been immersed deeply in writing and directing, he could no longer tell the difference between reality and fiction. He was a thirty five years young man who studied theater in London; ever since he returned home three years ago, and was moving in vicious circles. His name was Tariq and he said that he had too many lovers and that he could not even remember all their names or the time he had with them. All he wanted to remember that day was his last day on land before leaving the planet and heading deep into the bottom of the ocean in the no-return journey.

To Tariq, whose original name was Ramy, the Belly of the Whale with its mystery and surprises was superior to the dull real life that had driven him to the verge of suicide. Ramy had black eyes and a fair round face; he looked like a sun- colored Greek. A seasoned lover and womanizer, he could only see Laila as yet another beauty who was deeply lost in thoughts. The pride and strength that she attempted to show did not convince him. He could sense that she was mysterious and uncomfortable and that part of her refused the whole experience of Belly of the Whale.

They talked while having drinks; Tariq was eager to hear about Laila's story and to know how she got to Paradise. He asked her if she was happy and inquired about the reasons that made her join the journey. He knew beforehand that she would never tell him the truth; these were the rules of the game. She would be thrown into the sea for sharks to devour if she uttered anything about her reality; she would then be an example for the rest of the people. Belly of the Whale was their second and last chance to change their lives and to attain happiness; that was the real aim of the journey. In order to attain it and get the life they had always wished for, everyone turned their lies into actions. They were convinced that only happiness was their target; nothing was worthy of sorrow and they only got one chance to live that they should not waste.

Laila started to narrate her story; she said that she came from a poor family who lived in the mountain and that she only got the chance to live in the city for a brief period before joining Belly of the Whale. As she narrated, she hummed a folk song that she said, or maybe pretended, was her favorite. The lyrics went "Come on baby, take me away to heal my broken heart; I have had enough; why did your heart change and forgot me? I cannot believe it; you don't even talk to me". Ramy, who became Tariq in the journey, was amazed by her cleverness; she looked really happy humming that song. Could she really be that clever pretending to be someone other than herself?

This woman really astonishes me! Tariq, no Ramy, don't you ever go back to your old ways that led you to that strange journey; to Belly of the Whale. How did I get that idea? How did I dare to carry it out without thinking about the damage I could do to the lives of people who trusted me and followed my example? What is wrong with you Ramy? Why are you so reluctant and doubtful now? Everyone in Belly of the Whale is happy; I did not hear a single person complain; don't be a coward Ramy and finish off what you have started.

What about your story Mr. Handsome? Laila asked as she was thinking about Tamara; she did not even know what made her think of Tamara and imagine her like a faraway star in a faraway sky; she looked so far and unreachable. Adam! How did you dare Hala to leave him behind? How could you bring yourself to do it? What kind of mother you are? What a loving and affectionate mother! She suddenly felt like a little sparrow in a cage but managed to suppress her tears. Come on Hala! Be brave! Don't chicken out; you've got to finish what you have started. You were chosen for this mission, a divine mission that could change the path of the human race on earth and transfer humanity to a happier, more beautiful place. All you have to do is to make this experience a success. Don't worry as long as Mona is there to take care of you children. God bless you Mama and keep you safe. Oh God, but what if something wrong happens to her while I am gone? Only God had the might and strength! Remove these evil thoughts from your mind Hala; your mother blessed your decision and encouraged you to go; stop being a pessimist. Maybe all what you need now is some rest; you did not rest all day and it is almost four in the morning. Though Hala lived a very busy life, she never loved staying up late; she was a day-loving person who could never understand or appreciate staying up late. Be strong Hala! Do not surrender! The hall is still full with guests and the noise is deafening even to the sharks that surround the huge Whale ship. Beams of light started to penetrate the windows despite the darkness of the bottom of the ocean. What a beautiful sight, the weeds and the pearls shine in their shells! But Laila thought that witnessing a better future had turned into an unreachable dream. Tariq could not convince her to drink alcohol with him; she valued her integrity and could not risk being drunk. Or maybe that what she pretended to be, thought Tariq. We were supposed to pretend to be the opposite of who we really were and maybe that was why she always resisted his insistent invitations to share alcohol with him. That probably meant that her reality was just the opposite of what she pretended. Hala realized that she had just unconsciously refused alcohol and that was how she really felt about it. She started to count her mistakes; that was her first and maybe it was due to her exhaustion; all she needed was to get some sleep, even if it meant she had to lie down on the floor and sleep; nothing mattered to her anymore.

Ramy, now called Tariq has his own leisurely style of attracting girls to him; he enjoyed doing it unhurriedly and it brought him happiness to do so. No matter how strong headed a girl might be, she could never resist him; he was a Casanova. But with Laila, he could never feel anything at all, maybe it was due to the stress that came with arrangement of that mysterious journey that was both unpredictable and unguaranteed.

Part Three

RAMY KEPT WONDERING WHAT SALMA was doing in Belly of the Whale, with whom she was dancing and with whom she would be spending the night? She was his beloved and mistress and even though they were never connected in holy matrimony, he could not bring himself to believe that marriage was important in a sexual relationship based on love. Still, he did not know why he felt a burning in his stomach every time he imagined that she might fall in love with someone else. They loved each other and she should be faithful to him for life, and that applied to him too. He had repeatedly suggested a civil marriage in Cyprus but she insisted to have a church marriage, though he was a Muslim, thanks to God. Or maybe we should say he was a Muslim by identity only since his conventions and beliefs were always subject to change according to circumstances. He would sometimes fast in Ramadan, but refuses to do so many times; he rarely prayed but he was always charitable and helpful to whoever needed his help; he was good to his parents and he hated back biting. Salma my love! Where are you now? How can I find you among a thousand people? I know how clever you are in disguising yourself; we have been together for ten years and you could hide our relationship from everyone even your own parents. Laila left Tariq for a while to get the energy drink; she needed that bizarre liquid which was invented by a great specialist from the Association to help all inhabitants of Belly of the Whale stay awake forever. The drink contained wheat and honey and other energizing and anti-aging ingredients to help renew cells, keep the muscles strong and the mind alert, even if people stayed awake for hundreds of years. As Tariq gave the drink of life to Laila, his companion for the night, he wondered how long it had been since they entered Belly of the Whale. One minute in this place is equal to an hour outside it; we have already spent the first twenty four hours without even realizing how they were gone. There is no pollution here, no cars, no work, no cell phones and even no internet connection. Hoping to stay alert, Laila sipped her drink, little by little, and waited for the terrible vertigo that hit her head like an atomic bomb to go away. Come on Laila! Be brave! You have to get used to the new name; Laila is a more beautiful name than Hala and I have never even liked my original name anyway though it is a foreign name that suits my fair skin and blond hair. Laila suddenly shivered feeling that what she drank was a whole new life, not just a drink; that was a hell of a drink! A really exotic drink that made her tiredness disappear; she felt lighter that ever; there was no pain and she even did not feel her own weight. Was it some sort of sugar? No, no it did not taste like sugar; nor did it feel like nirvana. She felt like she was born a new; she became a totally new person brim with life and had no complaints whatsoever. That was how she felt.

Moments after having the drink, Laila and Tariq set out on a new dialogue, a dialogue that has nothing to do with what they have said before. It was like their unconscious minds had given way to the thoughts and ideas it kept buried without any restrictions or fears. A new story was launched, taking a totally new direction. Looking into Laila's blue eyes which had never been more beautiful, Ramy begged her to dance with him. "Let's dance, I have a burning desire to dance and speak with you!" Ramy asked pleadingly and she immediately accepted with a nod displaying her blond hair. She was more enthusiastic than him; she had never been more enthusiastic about dancing in her life; she did not even know she loved dancing to that extent. They both moved restlessly towards the dance floor, proceeding among the huge crowd of people who were intoxicated by the same drink and started to dance and whisper to one another. "I pity those who are still waiting for the drink and never got a chance to taste it! Cheers Laila, my beloved." Laila looked at Tariq and wondered if what she had heard was right or was she imagining it because of the effect of the drink. A few moments before he was telling her that he did not believe in love. Being the love expert and womanizer he was, he had found out that all love relationships were meaningless and pointless; they started and ended up with the feeling of boredom. Yes Laila, I am sure. Tariq was exceptionally intelligent and he definitely knew what he was saying. "Laila we have spent years together, don't you remember? I know you Laila, and you know me; my memory is recovered, what about yours?" "Laila, struck with amazement, stared at Tariq and cried: "Hagob! Is that really you?" The two lovers winked to one another as if they had never been apart. "How I missed you! I would have never felt happy until I found you. Where have you been? I have went to great lengths just wishing that we might meet by accident. Thank you God, we found each other again! Oh God, I have always had strong faith and here we are together; a miracle had just happened. Where have you been?" He said. "Where have **you** been?" Lucy answered, "I have been searching for you everywhere for years. How did you disappear from our neighborhood? And how did you come back, my love? I cannot believe my eyes Hagob!"

"Lucy, my sweetheart, I have to admit that I was the one who invented the energy drink but it never occurred to me that it would recover my memory, the sweet memories we had together and thought were gone forever like a paper kite lost on a neighbor's roof," he said. "Jacob, what do you mean? Is there any probability for a mistake in this journey? Are not you sure about your drink? What if everyone here remembered their lovers? What if they all knew one another in their previous lives and their minds still held the memories deep down! That would be a catastrophe! It will lead to chaos in our paradise! Aren't we supposed to be husbands and wives here? As far as I know the rule of the game necessitates that. I am surprised to know that you are not even married and that you substituted your wife with your lover. This is the first violation of the rules of the game! And here you are bringing me back to the world a long time after I died and resurrecting our time together, a time which I thought was gone with my death. To me you are Kamal! Kamal the one I lost when I was thirty five! This is another violation of the rules and how many other violations I will have to take! How many years have passed and how many lives have ended since then?" She said.

"Stop it sweetheart, please; I know I did you wrong but you realize how barbaric the holocaust was! I still remember how I hid among the trees in the garden of our house. How splendid is Armenia's sun! I don't want to feel sad sweetheart, not in Belly of the Whale. Do you feel the heat of the sun Lucy?" he said.

"Keep it down, here my name is Laila and I don't want my story to be revealed by anyone. Don't forget that we have to be under disguise; I don't want to end up into a shark's belly; I am quite happy and content to be in Belly of the Whale. But wait, does this mean you could invent the drink that brings you back to your lover and ignore the afterlife? Oh God! How could you do that? What diabolic abilities do you have? And how can we carry around that incomplete, distorted memory with big gaps that lacks the connection to whole chunks of our lives?" She said.

"I told you I never expected this to happen; let's wait and see what will happen to others; maybe it is just us that got back our old memories; maybe we are the exception to the rule." He said.

Both lovers recalled how everything was peaceful and calm when suddenly their houses and the houses of their neighbors collapsed; how they searched for human remains, toys or photos or anything to remind them of others. Was it an earthquake that no body but them felt? Was there anyone to blame for what happened? Hagob and Lucy then heard a soft wailing voice; they realized it was a girl. She was not just a girl in the common sense of the word; but a gorgeous beauty, an angel, a marvelous creation of God. Lucy's jealousy suddenly erupted like a volcano of lava; she did not know how to hide it. Oh God, how beautiful that wailing weeping girl was!!

Part Four

THAT CRYING GIRL HAD HER reasons to go into Belly of the Whale, Lucy thought, as she completed her story to the man dancing with her, the one without identity, the simple spontaneous man who called himself Sam. It must be one of his favorite names and that was why he chose it to accompany him to paradise. Marwa, the angle of mercy, the angle standing in front of them on the floor, or more precisely on the granite of Belly of the Whale. For a while Lucy could not decide whether it was made of marble or granite; she had to touch it with her soft hands three times to check what those beautiful pieces stuck together on the floor of paradise were made of. Never had she in her whole life seen something like that; it was neither marble nor granite; maybe it was made of onyx. It never occurred to her to ornament her luxurious apartment with that precious stone. Yes, I think it is onyx, she tells herself.

Trying to sooth Marwa, Sam askes her not to cry and adds that what happened to her and to her family was over and that her family were in a better place in heaven with God taking care of them. "Don't weep Marwa, maybe they can see us now and I am sure they are happy and content to see you here; don't be afraid sweetheart, I am here beside you and there is no death to take us apart and no earthquakes or buildings to collapse on our heads when we least expect; there are no merciless greedy traders who destroy even human lives to make profit. Do you want another drink? It is the elixir of life! Do you feel tired sweetheart? We are here to be happy; we have no time to waste on trivial problems; we have no work, no commitments, no mobiles or cars or planes and no access to media. We have no families even, nothing at all to care for but our happiness; we don't even have time to sleep and staying up will not hurt us."

"Excuse me Sam; I still need some time to be able to forget about my emotions; maybe our life on earth made me vulnerable to pain, cold and hunger; I just need a few days, or maybe years since I don't know how to count the Whale days compared to our regular days. How long have we been here Sam? I don't remember."

"We have been here for a year, I think Marwa. See, we did not feel it was a year. It feels like one night of endless dance for us. We don't know when it started or when will it end; it will never end unless we decide. If we do, God forbids, this will be our failure. We are happy as you can see; really happy and will never feel tired; all we need to do is to take the drink and our cells will do the rest for us; they will renew themselves automatically and keep us alive for ever."

Sam jerked up with a sudden feeling of intoxication and carried his angel-like bride to have some rest on a sofa that he had specially designed. He was a sculpture and painter who had a talent for designing furniture. He still remembered what the Chairman of the Association told him when he chose him for this job and how he expressed his admiration of his creative ideas and style of designing palaces and hotels with huge halls. He was honored to be chosen to design the furniture. His name will be immortalized not only for joining the experience of the Belly of the Whale but for designing its furniture as well.

Marwa looked at him with infatuated eyes, beckoning to him to finish narrating the story. When he said it all started a year ago was a year ago, she laughed because she did not know if it was a whale year or a normal year.

-A normal year of course sweetheart, we were still there on earth, angle

-This is amazing; you are a genius really, and you did all that in one year only? How could you?

-I did not executed the plan all by myself, Marwa; I specialized in wood works and it was my only task. The Chairman recruited a wonderful team of helpers, talented and skilled sculptures, and painters.

-Are they here with us on board of Belly of the whale? It is not fair to exclude them.

-Yes sweetheart; everyone who participated in making the ship got the chance to join; our Association is just; trust that. And maybe that is why there are a thousand people on board. The ship was designed for a thousand people, no more, no less. We will not have children and we will not die either. So just rest assured and be happy and let them take lead.

Marwa felt happy; her face radiated as it never did before.

-How strong is the effect of that drink! I yearn to recognize the one who invented it; he is a genius!

-Careful Marwa! I am starting to feel jealous, though I am sure that there is no jealousy, nor selfishness or rebuke on board of Belly of the Whale. This is the Utopia, the city of unlimited freedom; everyone does what he or she wants without limits or restrictions or supervision. Yes, we have deserved trust; the Chairman would not have risked choosing any substandard guests. We are the elite Marwa, we are God chosen. Have you ever thought about silk brocade?

-Sam, I swear I don't believe my eyes! Sofas made of fine silk brocade! How could you do that? Where did you get the fabric and who paid for it?

-Donations Sweetie; everyone who joined our paradise have given up their belongings with a written a formal waiver that was hidden in a place that only a few of the founders of the Association know.

-But this is not fair? What about the people they left behind on earth?

-Everything is under control sweetie; those people are multi-millionaires! Do you really want to know how much the sofas and the cushions cost? The wood and ornaments?

-No, my love, I don't. I still feel like a slave to money; maybe later when I get over my servitude to it. Don't forget that I came from a poor neighborhood and have fought to make money. In one of my panel discussions about women rights and child protection, I once referred to the power of money on us and how we worshiped money instead of God the Almighty.

-Yes, so you are a social activist?

Of course nothing of what Marwa had said about herself was right; maybe she chose that personality, studied it carefully before embarking on the Whale experience because she had wanted to be like that in reality. Sam reminded himself that everyone on board of belly of the whale had a fake story, or more. But he liked her assumed personality all the same; there was nothing wrong with that, he reminded himself. As long as we would never leave Belly of the Whale, I would interact with Marwa with my present personality and the emotions I feel for the present. Here, I am not my real self too, and only God knows who I really am. Who am I anyway? I have become a stranger even to myself: am I really the great sculptor who paved the floors with onyx and sewn the silk brocade linen? I don't want to remember. Marwa liked my sofa and I will keep it; it does not matter if I were a skilled upholster or a sculptor as long as I will never go back to my original work for the rest of my life. I have always wanted to be a sculptor, why not do it? Leonardo da Vinci is not superior to me. Come on, Calm down Sam! But who is that Sam anyway? What is wrong with you Samer? Have you really forgotten your real identity while pretending to be Sam? Don't be hard on yourself; why are you indignant now? Haven't you practiced how to live in Belly of the Whale for a long time and enjoyed a life that does not have any chances for distress? Forget that sinister day Samer and let it go. But how can I do that? How can I forget being overlooked? My name was deleted from the list of top students of my class in favor of another student just because I was poor, how can I get over that? I wished I had powerful relatives or someone to back me up; things would have been different for me. I would have been living in Rome or Paris or London or other capitals; I would have been touring the world now and letting the world know about me talent. I would have competed against that Leonardo da Vinci and had my paintings displayed in Louver. But you have accomplished a lot; you are such a talented and famous designer. Besides, it is too late for regrets now; you have left the whole world behind to live in Belly of the Whale. Don't you see justice in how things turned out for you? I've always wondered where that untalented person whom they favored over me? Nobody has heard about him ever since.

Part Five

WHAT A WILLOWY GRACEFUL FIGURE and a proud gait you have!? Where have you got that beauty Princess Hend? He said as he moved around her displaying his adoration as they danced slowly.

- Thank you for the complement my Prince Moataz. She answered and felt proud having been able to attract such a charming and handsome man. She remembered that old cottage, and how it all happened. She could not believe what happened up to the present moment. She was drawing by the sea at sunset and the view was wonderful.

I wish I could see my poor unfinished painting; the sun dove like a radiant ball of fire into the blue water and still retained its yellow color. And what a storm! The storm that turned my life upside down, but was the change for better or for worse? I think it changed my life both ways; what I suffered that night was unimaginable; I was swept away by the waves, or was it a tsunami actually? I have never before heard of the word; all I remember is that suddenly I could see nothing; I felt suffocated, and I was left on the branch of a tree before I fell on the roof of the old cottage. I can never forget the excruciating pain I felt then! I was raving, that's what he, Ali Eldeen, told me then after a week of losing consciousness. Oh God, how I miss you Ali Eldeen! How could we do what we did? How could we fell in love all of a sudden and how could our love grow like topsy and prevail the whole wide world. Then what happened to us? Why did we agree to part?

Why did we come to Belly of the whale? Where are you Ali Eldeen? And how can I recognize you among the disguised crowds who look exactly the same here? Oh Ali, my Sheikh, my Monk! How could you charm me that way? Do you think I will have another chance? Do you think I will get a chance here in this earthly paradise? I am confused! Is it on earth, or in heaven or in the water? It does not matter anyway. I have no family left; tsunami destroyed my family tree; I lost everyone. My pain and heartache are unbearable. My family have turned into Angles! I won angles residing now by God in heaven! What angles? What good is it to me? This was what I and Ali Eldeen disagreed about all the time. I never had faith; I was an atheist. I love drawing; I adore art and colors and I see God through them; nature is sacred to me because it is tangible. How did this Muslim Sheikh love me with the cross hanging from my neck, with my catholic beliefs: the father, the son and the Holy Spirit? How did our religions merged and melted forming our own scarlet pure endless anthem? Ours was not love it was madness, infatuation that surpassed all sorts of passion and adoration. I am still dazzled by the memory of this sheikh's love in which passion, asceticism and desire mingled. How could Sufism be manifested through excitement and pleasure and how could it still retain its spiritual peaceful core. I have done my best to bridge the gap between us and he repeatedly asked me why I wore the cross though I had no faith. I actually did not know the answer. I was obliged to have a faith; I believe faith is a need, not a choice. I love God and He loves me; I resort to Him and He never fails me; he has always been by my side. But I practice my prayers in my own different way. Churches suffocate me, the scent on incense frightens me and the sound of the bells irritate me. I have always prayed to my Lord through colors, whether joyful or gloomy; isn't that a prayer too? Won't my prayers count? Ali Eldeen escaped deeply into himself; he was afflicted with a calamity, a lover who had no faith and he had to do something about it. "You have to wear the veil, it is better for you; look at your seducing auburn hair! I won't blame men for desiring you. Even I, the Sufi hermit could not resist your charm and I fell into your trap, how can I blame them? Cover up your beauty woman; you are torturing me; have mercy on me!"

Oh Ali, how grateful I felt when you agreed to accompany me to Belly of the Whale! Where are you now? I would do anything just to find you here so that we can live without falsify or deception. There are no religious barriers or restrictions here; nothing can take us apart.

Ali, being the hermit with the great spiritual energy, managed to recognize her. Batla was his beloved and he could distinguish her among a million women through the special scent of amber that characterized her. But he would not utter a word; he would not risk her life since she was all his life. He would not cause her to be thrown into the sea and watch her being devoured by sharks; he could not take such a thing. He was determined not to go near her or allow her to approach him in any way; he would guard her and make sure she was always safe. That was the reason he came to Belly of the Whale in the first place. He was never convinced with this promiscuous adventure; he came for her and he worshiped Allah in Belly of the Whale, there was nothing to preventt him and he would never stop praying.

Do you really want to pray Ali Eldeen? Are you really a committed worshiper? What brought you to that place? How did you abandon life once and for all? Did you do all that for her? Yes, she was the reason. She was my young beloved Saa'da who left me to get married to someone else, to a man as old as her father. But you know it was not her decision; yes I do know, and that was why I punished myself because I was not man enough to protect her. How could I have reacted like a man when I was only sixteen and had no money of my own? Poor Saa'da she had no moment of peace in her life with that old man! She was as miserable as a lush rose in a field of old thorns. She cried her heart out and tore out her long black hair and all I could do was showering her lips with kisses. Oh my broken wings and fallen dreams! I was so depressed that I refused to wake up. It has been a long time since that sad story ended. In that terrible ordeal it was my religion that gave me patience, thank Allah. I am a believer; this word has such a powerful influence. I am a believer; I am a believer; I am a believer. I have practiced saying the words until I became a true believer at heart. I feel God is there in my heart, but what about Batla? How can I de-root and purify myself from her? Help me Allah; I am no longer capable of remaining chaste.

-"Prince, you did not tell me your name!" Batla swayed as she softly finished off her question: "do you want me to guess it?"

-"Don't bother Princess Hend, my name is Jalal."

That game of picking names is really something! I have always been a genius in choosing names, Fadel tells himself. When the Chairman asked me to take care of the details of disguising, names were the first thing I thought about. I deleted the real names of the guests of Belly of the Whale and removed them from the list of suggested names. Then the guests picked their new names from the list and it was a first come, first serve process so the ones who came first had wider choices. Once chosen, a name was deleted from the list. Then came the idea of adding more names in case the guests wanted to have more than one personality in Belly of the Whale.

-"Yes princess, my name is Jalal and I will tell you my story."

The name does not matter since I will not be telling her my real story. If my name were Yasser, it would have changed anything. I will not be telling my true story so things will not get complicated. She might even be my wife! Who knows? No, no, that is so unreasonable, how can I not know my wife? Or maybe it is possible not to recognize my wife since I do want to forget about her. My poor, beautiful wife! I have hurt her so much! What is wrong with you Yasser? Do you love her? You have always pretended you did not! You have tortured and humiliated her and falsely accused her and here you are yearning for her? And here in Belly of the Whale! What is this nonsense! Let me concentrate now and focus on princess Hend, the one I liked and chose to accompany me endlessly…

-So what is your story my Prince Jalal? - Listen Hend, I was a senior engineer; I have constructed many palaces and skyscrapers.

- Then, what happened?

- Then I had that strange disease, a muscle-eating virus that no one had ever heard of. It could destroy every muscle in the body, even the heart muscles themselves! I had suffered for a long time before I was cured. You know even diseases have their own budget. It was not just about suffering, since health insurance does not cover anything but the flue. I have knelt to the Lord asking him to cure me, even though I used to be a carouser and an alcoholic. Poor Feryal, you have endured me and put up with my anger which I vented on you for no reason. That poor woman underwent so much for me. Maybe that was why I agreed about Belly of the Whale as a way of paying back to her since she was the one who asked for it after she joined that strange Association. How could she convince me? Feryal had such an irrefutable argument! Women are subtle and cunning. I wonder where she is now. And with whom? Is she happy or just stuck in the middle like me? Come on Yasser! Be brave! Here is your princess Hend.

"Do you mean the malignant disease?" Hend asked

"No, my princess. Even malignant diseases can be cured now but mine was a totally new disease. It was the outcome of pollution and ozone hole, as I was told back then. I don't know if there is a cure for it now since we are here in the Belly of the Whale, not knowing what is happening outside. We don't even know how long we have been here and how this period affected the progress of medicine on earth. Hend, I have a feeling of dissatisfaction about life here and on land too.

Trying to calm him down, Hend swallowed her own fears and pain and answered:

Don't worry about these negative feelings my prince. We are happy here so don't think any farther. It is too late anyway since we are on a no return journey and regret won't help anymore.

But how? I thought I could always call the Chairman whenever I felt desperate; it was an implicit part of the deal. I never thought that the journey was eternal; I have hidden a bit of hope about the prospect of change deep into my heart. Don't you think we can change?

-Jalal, you are a bit confused. All you need is to relax, Please don't bother yourself thinking.

Part Six

INTERNET-OBSESSED KHALID INTERRUPTED THE PRIVACY of Jalal and
Hend, shouting at the top of his voice. Everyone around suddenly kept
silent and listened to what he said. They were astounded, fearing that
Khalid might remove his mask and decide to end the game and set himself
free. Why did they all have the same thought? Did they all implicitly want
to do the same and be free? Did they feel bored? Khalid's scream baffled
all of them; they could never imagine that a colleague, who might be the
husband of any of the ladies on board, would end up tossed into the sea
for sharks to eat in front of their eyes. Instead, Khalid amazed them with
a loud and detailed explanation of all the equipment on board, the sound
equipment and cameras that were spread everywhere. He complimented
all those on board of the Whale; all those who signed a written and sealed
contract that was kept in a secret information bank, a contract in which
they approve to be filmed anytime and under all conditions. No one of
them ever cared what would happen after the journey since they will never
go back or see anyone they used to know before.

Soon enough quiet was restored to Belly of the Whale when
everyone was sure that Khalid was only playing a role that he perfected
and that he did not think about removing the mask of his disguise.
All what he had done was a reaction to one technical question that
someone asked him about how to operate one of the specialized
devices. Instead of answering the question, he gave general and vague
explanations that made everyone feel bored; nobody believed him since
they were all well-educated people who could read between the lines.

Mayada whispers into Khalid's ears "what a genius you are! How could you deceive them? You are the one who really installed the devices, I do believe you after what you said. You have explained to me before very precisely everything that eliminates any doubts that you could be the one who designed and installed the appliances. Khalid you are such a shrewd person! How did I fall in love with you?"

Raa'id, who pretends to be Khalid, remembered the old days and reminisced about his excessive love of computers, to the point of ecstasy. He remembered the image he adored, the illusion, the virtual personality that he loved through the internet. How had she managed to deceive him, to convince him? He was infatuated with her to the point he could not believe himself, being the man belonging to the digital world. He never thought he could love someone that much. Being the man of numbers he was, he would never have trusted her if he had not put her to the test many times, and every time she proved her good intentions until they finally met.

Discussing Belly of the Whale was the reason they met. To see her, he had to spend a lot of money, to go to the end of the world and to issue several entry visas, including transit ones. The time we live in was so hard on someone who carried the name "Raa'id".

Do you regret it now Raa'id? Don't you miss your computer and your solitude in a dark room and the pictures of beautiful women on your walls? I have never felt better than I feel today; I am in paradise since Mayada is the one my heart chose. My choice was out of sheer instinct, without any other considerations; it was a choice based on the chemistry between us. The Chairman had that one condition for entering paradise: to be honest in our feelings.

Mayada looked at Khalid passionately and lamented the old days when she was called Salima, and nicknamed Soso. She had always felt sick because her servant had been slowly poisoning her for ten years in several ways whether secretly or openly.

Salima said that their decision to leave behind their pointless trivial life and go to Belly of the Whale was a sophisticated one. Her children had already grown up and it was not easy to keep living with them anymore. Besides, their society did not tolerate splitting the family or living apart. Their life together lately was empty; a servant served hookah and they did some fooling around, that was all.

Khalid is the right person for me; he has those special vibes that I have never felt before. Mayada whispered into his ears "Khalid what if we get bored from the recorded songs we listen to here?" he answers: "Don't ever mention the word boredom Mayada. There is no boredom in Belly of the Whale! You will never get bored; I promise. You will listen to things that neither you nor anyone else has never imagined, don't you trust me? I have thought carefully about that beforehand and made sure we have unlimited reserve of new songs. Just relax and enjoy; this is all I want you to do. Would you like another drink?" he said. "Yes, please Khalid. That drink of life makes me feel at least ten years younger". She answered. She knew that she was young and that getting married when she was young was what made her feel old and slack. The beauty of Belly of the Whale was that it removed all traces of misery and age; there was room only for ever-renewed and permanent youth.

Oh Lord, please give me patience, help me forgive and forget the past. Oh Lord, grant me happiness and help me enjoy that beautiful journey that I deserved after all the problems I suffered in my life. God, please protect me from all evils in Belly of the Whale. You are the most Merciful and the all Forgiver. That was the supplication that Mayada started and ended her day with. She would repeat it over and over again when she felt a bit bored and when monotony started to permeate her life. That was why she wanted to ask a crazy question: she wondered if she were a machine, a love making machine only?! But soon enough, she refuted the idea.

I am a human being, I am a human being, I am a human being. I want to live; I want to live happily. It is my right; I deserve to pamper myself. I have been wronged for so long; I have been so hard on myself never cared for it until it exploded and repelled even against me and led me here. Is there a place farther than this to run away to? Oh my God, how did I miss the idea of escape? Is it true that all of us here are only trying to escape? But from what do and towards what? Premonitions and more premonitions!

"Give me another drink Khalid please; I feel dizzy" she said. "Calm down sweetheart; it is only normal; don't forget we're in the middle of the sea" Khalid said in an attempt to, calm her down without even knowing the reason why she was worried. He had noticed that she had been absent minded for a long time.

Part Seven

"SWAY, SWAY MY WILLOWY BOASTFUL Shaima. How charming you are my tall brunet. Keep bending, swaying and indulging yourself. How I desire you and yearn to have you." It was only natural that he, master of sweet words, said those words to Shaima who looked like a beautiful desert deer as she danced to the popular song (U Dana Dan Elly Dana). She came from the heart of the desert carrying with her all the love and infatuation radiating from its sand. Shaima was the queen of all queens, the glorious drop-dead beauty of the concert with a slender body like a palm tree carrying ripe dates and cheeks the color of bronze wheat under October sun. Mourad was aware that everyone in Belly of the Whale were looking at him with envious eyes; but she had chosen him; he was the one her heard desired! No Mourad, do not compare her to Sicilia who was nothing but a machine, a sex machine that knew nothing about love itself. Her cruel disposition was what ruined our relationship; I do not deny having loved her; I adored her with all my heart but her jealousy slaughtered our love and destroyed her and me as well. She was afraid to get pregnant lest she should spoil her graceful figure, that daughter of Pashas had always fought fiercely to convince me that having children is not a necessity; that our pleasure was the most important thing; that we must enjoy ourselves to the full. She made sex a daily practice and a duty that the toughest and most vigorous of men would not be able to bear.

I am happy to have deserted the house in which desire lurked around every corner like explosives and emotions were fossilized. All she cared for was to exhaust my energy so that I will not be able to cheat on her; she never realized that what she did was only a workout of renovating my energy and that the restrictions which she thought would attract me to her actually pushed me away with the same power. The strength she showed was but a cover of her inherent weakness, of her tortured and distorted soul and her lack of self-confidence. I do not even want to remember my name; I am all through with her anyway; I am Mourad and I will never be Sameh again. From now on I am Mourad. Oh God, how long have we been here in Belly of the Whale? I no longer remember. I have drank a whole lot of the drink of life that can revive me for hundreds of times. What a miracle! Being in Belly of the Whale is just unbelievable! It is wonderful! I do not want to know how things are going with her; I do not even yearn to find out with whom she spends the night; I am fed up with her and that is what I am sure about.

You unbeatable resourceful Shaima! How did this bizarre idea cross your mind? How audacious you are! How could the housemaid impersonate her princess? But why not? They have always been inseparable (just like a dancer and her personal servant). And Shaima was one hell of personal servant! She never left the side of her mistress or missed any of her travels, she escorted her on shopping sprees in fancy shops and chose the best of products; she had her mistress's hairdresser and makeup artist do her hair and makeup just like a real princess. She had mastered the game and lacked nothing but having high origins.

I don't like the name Nouria; I am Shaima now and will never again be Nouria. Long live the Whale which raised me to the level of a princess! Long live the Whale and the drink of life! But what about your sweetheart, Nouria? The prince who secretly loved you and sacrificed all dear and precious things for you? How could you give him up and throw him into the arms of the beautiful women in Belly of the Whale? Nothing matters! He is boring; he does not belong to my class anyway. He had taken what he needed from me and gave me things in return and that is all about it. Wake up Shaima! Stop that nonsense. You are liberated; you are free. Take one more drink and you live a hundred more lives. How long have it been since we came here? Oh God, I do not remember any more. Maybe it has been at least a hundred years since this is my fourth drink and one drink makes you live a whole life. What a beautiful life of endless staying awake and vigilance and nothing more. "Where are you my King Mourad? Don't you want to listen to my story? I have listened to you attentively as you narrated how you travelled to China in search of knowledge. Don't you want to know the stories I have hidden for you? I originally was a nymph!" She laughed and swayed in a frivolously amorous manner. "I was a princess, haven't you noticed my manners?" Mourad answered as he held her tight not bothering about where she came from or of what descent she was. He answered: "But I haven't seen you before? Were you in exile or what?" All he cared about was a happy life that was about to start. But nosey Nouria, who was fond of adventures and new discoveries, was upset; she does not like his attitude. She had been able to intrude into the palaces of kings and princes, not considering the opinions or attitudes of her tribe or phratry. She did not deny that she loved her family but at the same time, she disavowed them for the sake of money and fame. No matter how powerful they become, they would never be leaders, unless of their own tribe, or an opposing clan if they were clever enough to raid their tents and enslave their women. They will never own palaces or cars; what do they need card for anyway being the wandering Bedouins they are? Their tents with the tranquility and serenity they inspire, however, have been always a theme for poets. Despite everything, she still sometimes yearns to be part of their late gala dinners in the desert, to the smell of coal burning on the stoves. She does not deny her love of charcoal grilled lambkin and gravy. How wild you are! No matter how hard you try to be Shaima, you will always love seeing blood running from the slaughter of sheep; love of blood runs in your system. Admit it! Admit that you are tribal at heart; admit that you will not be able to change yourself no matter how hard you tried. Your poor prince husband who ended up in Belly of the Whale just to satisfy and please you had brought you the best foreign teachers but it was all in vain. You could never change your disposition; deep down you are a mere Bedouin; you will never be civilized no matter how hard you tired. To change her frustrated mood, Shaima goes for another drink. "I am Shaima, I am Shaima, I am Shaima", she repeats to herself trying to make her unconscious mind accept the idea.

Mourad was happy when she asked for one more drink since he himself was not satisfied yet. He still desired her and he wanted her to be happy and excited and motivated, not restless or bored or complaining of being tired from excessive love making. He hurried up and filled her glass and she sipped it with a desire that matched his desire for her. She was fond of love making and could never conceal her desire, or maybe better say, her wildness, her ardent desire and temptation which made her really happy. Her happiness was never complete until she spent a long night of love-making. If she was given a ring or a diamond set as present from her prince husband she would reward him back by making love so that he would give her more presents and so on. That was the sort of life Shaima had; a life that suited her gypsy origins.

Part Eight

MUDDLED THOUGHTS SPUN AND SWIRLED in Basma's mind when she remembered her luxurious extravagant life before joining crazy adventure in Belly of the Whale. She used to have four lovers, not just one; she had three houses instead of one and instead of one boring nonstop party, she had a hundred short varied ones. How could they convince her to join? How did Sarya give up all what she had and leave everything behind? How did she became satisfied with one lover and one party and one endless night? Basma drank many cups of the drink of life just to boost her mood. She had never liked that secluded life; what they called an eternal life was but a cave life to her. She had to choose her alleged lover to be able to join that game and he looked like the right person at first. Basma was not a teenager; she was a grown woman in her thirties who often talked about her experience. She suffered from depression as a result of her huge wealth and emptiness of her life. Despite the big number of her lovers, she suffered an unprecedented sense of alienation and introversion that she would not admit to anyone except her psychiatrist. He had to keep her secret; and she could sue him if he disclosed it. She eagerly told him about her love stories and her nights of love making. She had given herself the right to be in a relationship with four men at a time just like a husband; she granted herself the same rights like a man[6]. She also

---

[6] Muslim men are granted the right to be married to four women at a time but under special conditions.

added more flavor and variety to her love making by sleeping with some gorgeous girls; there was nothing wrong with a bit of experimenting. Basma was addicted to drugs; alcohol was not enough anymore to silent her banging head that was loaded with exhausting love appointments. She did not orgasm easily and needed hours and hours of violent love making. Every time she got an orgasm, she felt the need for more; her thirst for sex was endless and unquenchable and often lead to depression that ended only by a new morphine dose.

She was wandering aimlessly around in the golf club that autumn day when she met the Chairman of the Association who seduced her though she was the one who had already seduced most men and women in the city. Basma did not have children because her husband was infertile, infertile and wealthy and that was what really mattered. Oh God, I wonder with whom he is sleeping now. Is there any woman who would endure his coldness? Come on Basma! Stop it! Do not be malicious and wish him luck and maybe then God will help you too. You came here to heal; to be purged and cleansed from the clutches of your evils and your divergences. Is that true Sarya? I do not understand myself and I do not even know my own needs. "What is wrong my darling", her alleged lover Riad asked, "Why are you turning your face away? Come on, look at me! Oh, I can see tears in your eyes that refuse to fall down!"

Basma no longer wanted to have the drink of life; she did not want her new name; she has always been Asmaa and never Basma[7]; how could she smile when she had been depressed all her life? Basma did not answer Riad's question, so his mind started to wander outside the scope of the Belly of the Whale. Damn that Whale cage! He had thought it would bring him eternal happiness! I am fed up with the energy drink; I feel like a bull racing in a rodeo in Spain! I am fed up with the loathsome sex; my girl is so avaricious; she is never satisfied and I am not a robot; I am a human being and I have feelings; I don't

---

[7]   The word pronounced "basma" means "smile" in Arabic, hence she refuses the name that does not reflect her personality.

function on electricity! I need to breath; I am suffocated! Where are you Rabia? And with whom are spending the night? Are you happy Rabia? How I miss you and yearn for our little nest by the sea, the chalet where we used to spend sweet nights! I wish those days would come back. Oh, what is wrong with you Mokhalad? Why did you pick "Riad" for your new name? I can no longer bear that name either. What is wrong with you Mokhalad? Why are you so pessimistic? Do not let her infect you with her bad moods and her craziness. But how can I cope with her? I cannot break up with her; she is my partner according to the oath of the Whale. What is the oath and what is the whale anyway? Who made up this big lie and made the rules and the conditions? I will find a way out of this dilemma; I cannot take it anymore. Mokhalad thought about being open about his opinion but in a prudent and cautious way. He thought carefully before uttering a word, hoping to get some pity out of the one with rock- hard heart who cared about nothing but exhausting love- making. Every story has another half that we do not know, another hidden face which might be the real one. "We might come across people who are willing to listen attentively to the other half of our story; I am still waiting to listen to the rest of yours; I am all ears," Mokhalad said to the scowling gloomy Basma who responded to his wish only by keeping her mouth shut so as not to admit a true word about her life. Truth detecting machines were all over the hall and whistles would announce the disclosure of Sarya's personality and she would be thrown into the ocean. Sarya took her decision to keep stickling and going on with the game. "I will not utter a word; I will not die; I do not want to die."

What an artful wily woman you are Sarya! How could you keep your poor husband in the dark all the time? How could that hard-hearted, husband of yours not notice this? Yes he was infertile! Barren! But why did you keep living with him? Why did not you think about leaving him? Why did not you abandon him? The only thing you could do was cheating on him! Do you really hated him? Why do you look so confused now? Is that because you have lost him and lost other things with him? Maybe you have just started to see things as they really are and to admit your crime. That infertile husband of yours never wronged you; he did nothing but pampering you! But maybe he too had other lovers and I could not find out. There is no need for regret now! I have taken my decision and what is done is done; it is all over; I came here to set roots for myself; I could not do that on land. Here there is no room for changing partners every night and moving from one night club to another or wandering about the streets looking for more victims. Wake up Sarya and stop torturing yourself!

But what about that cold insensitive partner? How could he not notice I was a drug addict? This is beyond reason. He is evil, evil and cold, this all I believe he is. How I hated him and I still do; I hate all men; I hate women too. I am malicious and I do not want to be cured of malice; I envy anyone who is happier than me; I cannot do anything but hate and envy. Oh God, I cannot forgive; I am spiteful, selfish and possessive and this is who I am! I cannot change myself; I desire destruction; I want to destroy everything; comprehensive destruction is what I seek.

Part Nine

KITCHENS OF BELLY OF THE Whale were close to the great hall, the dance floor and the dining rooms with the buffets and the restrooms for men and women. A hundred of the most experienced and renowned chefs and waiters from all over the world were brought to work there. They believed in the cause and considered the journey a humane mission. So they sacrificed their professional careers and came with the guests to the bottom of the ocean to cater for their endless needs; they cooked and served appetizers, main courses, desserts that no one has ever imagined. This army of chefs had absolute faith in the cause of Belly of the Whale which made them write and sign and seal contracts in which they vow to never complain about working around the clock to come up with unprecedented wonderful cuisine and garnish. If they felt tired, they would have the drink of life which provides endless energy and they would alternate shifts so that the guests could enjoy their nonstop party. Waiters and room service staff also enjoyed the privileges of the party of love and pride since Belly of the Whale contracts ensured social justice to all.

A cleaning staff member might fall in love with one of the beautiful ladies in Belly of the Whale, and according to rules of the game, that was permissible. All residents of Belly of the Whale were equal; enjoyment and desire were the only criteria to judge people on board. The Chairman of the Association has chosen the elite; they were distinguished in every manner; they loved their work and mastered whatever they did; they were reliable and academically excellent and as such, they were the pride of everyone who knew them. A chef was equal to a doctor or a hairstylist or a nurse or a dancer; they were all special and successful in whatever they did. And now there was plenty of time to dance; there was only dance and love on Belly of the Whale.

The gorgeous lady who chose the chief cook to be her lover and preferred him to all other men sat by herself at the bar drinking while he took care of the food in one of the fantastic kitchens of the Belly of the Whale. He enjoyed the tastes and garnishing methods that made every dish look like a work of art. Manaz, sitting alone for the time, seized the chance to reexamine her memory which had fallen apart because of the energetic drink of life. She had started to feel how important her memory was despite all what she had suffered back then before coming to Belly of the Whale. Manaz admitted that she had loved Edward, the chief cook of Belly of the Whale, and that she liked the idea of being in a relationship with a man who did not belong to her religion or come from a similar background like hers. She no longer needed to justify herself and relieved her from the perpetual need to prove herself as an obedient woman in a strict society. Edward was characterized by transparency and non-vulgarity, which were beautiful traits. He tried to pronounce Arabic after she taught him some of the words that she loved. But she also spoke his foreign language, the one she liked and mastered since she was a graduate of a foreign university. Manaz never felt that Edward had hidden memories in his heart; she did not try to ask him about his real name or whom he had left behind. She never noticed his confusion and his search for the partner that he had wholeheartedly given to Belly of the Whale. That night, unlike never before, Manaz had a desire to search for Mokhalad, her poor husband who never doubted her; she yearned for him without even knowing the reason. She tried to analyze her own situation that night: Edward was busy cooking and she had nothing to do but sipping the drink of life; it was the chance of lifetime to think rationally so that she might find out something new, something that motivated her to go on. She no longer felt the same pleasure she had in the beginning of the journey; despite all the energizing drinks and the new songs. Wake up Rabee'a? What is wrong with you? Do you really want to go back to the many men you used to know? You came to Belly of the Whale seeking redemption and purification and to prove that you have given up your promiscuity; you chose a foreigner who would accept you in case your secret was one day disclosed. Who is that Edward? Is he really a foreigner or is he the son of the desert like me and pretending to be otherwise? Why not? Maybe he was born to foreign mother and an Arab father and that was why he looked like a foreigner. But why are you so confused Rabee'a or are you Manaz? I no longer know who I am.

Mozafar, the supervisor of the cleaning staff, approached Manaz in an attempt to exploit the time his sweetheart Dr. Sakina spent with a sick lady who complained from stomachache. The pain might be due to an over dose of the energy drink, or due to unexpected pregnancy. The Chairman of the Association had promised them that there would be no pregnancy in Belly of the Whale since the natural environment did not support reproduction. "You will live in an environment that originally does not cater for human life," was what he said that day.

Mozafar introduced himself to the gorgeous Manaz and she was happy to talk to a new face, or rather, a new mask. Though he knew the rules of the game that entail no betrayal, nor cheating nor back stabbing, he proposed that they drink a toast to their new friendship.

Rabee'a regained her appetite for new men; she felt a huge desire to end up having a night of love-making, followed by another. She did not know that her experience in Belly of the Whale failed to change her nature. She was still Rabee'a, the woman who loved to have sex with many men and who was born not to ever feel satisfied.

Mozafar felt a tweak of guilt when Manaz excused herself to go the rest room and fix he make up. He was lucky to have Sakina; she was a renowned doctor but she was modest and humble enough to be in a relationship with a cleaning supervisor, despite all the talent and appeal he enjoyed with women. H had enough knowledge and culture that enabled him to attract any woman, no matter who she was. But Sakina was very special; she was different from all other women, a perfect lady in all the sense of the word. When she came to Belly of the Whale, she came for a humane cause; she knew that no one could guarantee that the residents would be in good health, no matter what kind of insurance or guarantees they had. She admitted that piece of information one time when she was away from the truth detecting machines.

Part Ten

A MIRACLE HAPPENED: THE RESPECTFUL LADY whose alleged name is Ma'ally had fallen in love with the one who calls himself Mobarak and she got pregnant. Refusing to leave her suffer by herself, Mobarak accompanied her to the clinic. How did she become pregnant when he was infertile? He had always wished to have a son to carry his named when he lived on land; he longed for an heir to handle his huge wealth, the wealth that Sarya had always disliked on the pretext that she was deprived from having children. He had visited many notable doctors and they all confirmed that he was infertile; it could not be possible that Sarya had bribed them all to say so! What happened then? Did Ma'ally cheat on me with one of the men in Belly of the Whale? No, no, no, it cannot be; I was always by her side; I did not leave her alone for a moment since we came to the ship. What will I do now when I am forbidden to say the truth about myself? How can I tell Dr. Sakina that I am infertile and that I doubt this pregnancy and my fatherhood of the coming son? Is it possible that the energy drink had helped with my sexual ability and boosted it up? And what can we do with the child in this place? How can we take care of it in such an environment that is not fit for life in the first place? How will the baby grow or go to school? Who will teach him and how can we find him a job or a female partner? We have tailored this ship just to suit us and never thought beyond that! Do I really want to have children by Ma'ally? Who is Ma'ally in the first place? Will I ever get to know her for who she really is? I have always wanted to have a child by Sarya; do I still love her? Will she be happy for me if she knew that I could have a child? How will she react? How will she justify that? Will she accept it? Will she forgive me? Will I be able to forgive her lies and her pretentions and the lies of my doctors about my infertility? How can I do that? I cannot think anymore.

The three of them discussed the baby and the pregnancy. Ma'ally pled to Dr. Sakina to tell her that it was a false pregnancy; she did not want children; she did not know that man. "It is only a game; all this life is merely a game, an illusion; I don't want him to be the father of my child; I don't accept him as a husband, please understand Doctor," she begged Dr. Sakina. Mobarak heard what Ma'ally said; he was not annoyed in any way; he himself felt the same since he was infertile. How could she be pregnant by him? And in Belly of the Whale too? He did not want that baby, even thought he had waited for it all his life; he did not want it. "Please doctor, help us; we don't want it; do whatever you can; you are in charge here, so be up to it," he said to Sakina as he ended the discussion.

Ma'ally was taken to her room on a stretcher stained with blood. She was bleeding after the abortion of the prodigy baby who was conceived against all odds. Dr. Sakina could do nothing to stop it nor could specify a particular reason for the bleeding. She said it might be because the patient was at a great depth under the sea. She asked Ma'ally to rest and take pills for bleeding but it was in vain.

Mobarak never left Ma'ally's side; he was not in the least interested in the perpetual party being held outside. He calmed her down and promised her another child when she got better, in another place after they manage to leave that hell of a place called Belly of the Whale. He had already started to think about ways to escape but soon Ma'ally got worse and lost consciousness so he hurried to get Dr. Sakina. But it was too late since Ma'ally had already died because of a virus she contracted during the abortion. This was what Dr. Ramsy said later. Getting rid of her corpse was very easy; sharks were all around the ship and everyone could see them. The pretexts to toss her into the sea was even easier; the truth detectors had caught her telling the truth and she had betrayed her lover and admitted that the baby was not his and that she had been raped by one of the masked men in the rest room on the night that her lover left her alone to check on the engines of the ship.

Mobarak was deeply depressed after Ma'ally's death; he had known nothing real about her except for the fact that she was raped on Belly of the Whale and ended up between the jaws of sharks right before his eyes. According to the rules of Belly of the Whale, he was entitled to choose another lady to be his partner for the rest of the party, on the condition that she and her original partner agree. There was a limited number of ladies and it was not possible to clone another man or woman. In that case they would have to share love and have group sex.

Days pass by, or maybe years, and Mobarak could psychologically recover at the hands of a glamourous lady whose original partner had started to feel bored by their unending love. He believed that accepting a new partner gave him a good chance to go back on the stupid vow he took when he first came to the ship of death, which he had then believed to be some sort of Noah's arch.

Mobarak did not care at all about Mayada's past, or the past of their partner Khalid; his situation was different from others because he was a left behind partner and deserved punishment. He did not want to listen to Khalid's stories about his infatuation with the internet and the digital world which led him under the sea in a sinking ship that was supposed to be a savior to all humanity. He did not care about the many times Mayada's servant had poisoned her; he had outgrown the feelings of happiness or melancholy and entered into a numb zone of feeling nothing at all. He was the only one who knew his own past and did not want to share it with anyone; he even did not want to remember it. What if the child was really his? What if for some reason Ma'ally could not tell the truth for fear of being tossed to sharks? She had gone to the sharks all by herself after rape and abortion.

Like Khalid and Mayada, Mobarak experienced moments of ecstasy, moments that he had never experienced before. He never knew that group sex could be fun, the idea never occurred to him though had known many beautiful women and fallen in love many times. Poor Sarya, she had never known anything about my adventures with women. I sometimes wonder how a woman not discover that her husband was cheating on her. I have always been baffled by Sarya, by her calm face that concealed many things I could never know about her. Are you happy Sarya here in Belly of the Whale? But he had started to feel bored, like Khalid and Mayada. Sometimes he was unable to feel the pleasure or maybe he did not want to at the time? Or is it that he had stopped feeling at all? He could not decide how he felt about anything; the only thing he was sure about was that he was unhappy.

Mozafar, the cleaning staff supervisor, who was originally the Billionaire Maher and Hala's husband and father of Adam and Tamara, also felt the same way. He longed to meet his children and though he had tried tirelessly not to think about them, his yearning for them increased every day. He no longer cared about Hala; she had always been so demanding and confused and had never known what she really wanted. She might not like the idea of escaping from Belly of the Whale. He might not even be able to recognize her since everyone on board were disguised and they failed to recognize themselves anymore. The idea of escape had crossed his mind may times; he once thought that he could hide in a trash bag and be thrown into the ocean but he lacked the courage to do it. Even though he was a good swimmer, he could not be sure that he would survive; he was in the bottom of the ocean thousands of kilometers away from the surface.

Maher recalled that the first volunteer job he had as a student was cleaning streets. He never belonged to a poor family but he was interested in scouting during school and he was happy to do it; it helped him see another world and move away from the luxury and riches of his family. He had always wanted to change; boredom was his biggest fear since he grew up and even after he got married to Hala who was the beauty queen of Lebanon, or so he thought back then. On Belly of the Whale he saw ladies who were a hundred times more beautiful than Hala and exceeded her in femininity and intelligence. But women were no longer enough reason for him to stay trapped in that prison. He preferred collecting the garbage in his city and its suburbs to staying on board. He wanted to leave that place to see his children; he wanted to go back to his apartment and be able to sleep. He did not sleep since he had came because the strange drink kept him alert, even if he fell asleep. He was on the verge of madness; he could not bear it anymore. I must go out of here; I have to go out alive for my children; I want my life and I need it. Maher took his decision and would find a way out no matter how much would that cost. But how? Everyone on board were extremely wealthy; nobody needed a bribe. What are my points of strength and what are their points of weakness? How can I convince them that we must go back?

Part Eleven

Nouria had a hobby: cooking and she had a little secret: she loved eating a special kind of truffles that is called "Faqe" in the Arabian Peninsula. It is a fungi-like plant that sprouts naturally in the Sahara after winter and its growth is related to thunder and lightning. Nouria, who called herself Shaima, had another hobby: having sex in the kitchen. She was ashamed of this hobby, but she was so used to it. Maybe the reason behind that was that she had been a maid servant to the real Shaima, Princess Shaima whom she poisoned day after day for years to steal her husband the prince. But after the death of real Shaima, she found out that the Prince was in love with another girl; he was never hers before or after Shaima. That was why she left the palace and pretended to be Princess Shaima and played that role cleverly enough to convince Sheikh Mash'aal, the very wealthy and powerful man, that she was the real Shaima and that she had to pretend to be dead to escape the injustice of her tribe, even when she was inside the palace. Then, the Chairman of the Association was impressed by her high standard and invited her to join this no-return journey. She could convince her husband Sheikh Mash'aal to join her; the reason he accepted remained a secret that he only knew.

Nouria went into the kitchen several times and observed Edward closely as he chopped the vegetables or ordered his assistants to do so. She enjoyed the smell of grilled fish before tasting it; Edward was so clever in mixing added flavors. The forgiving Mourad, whose original name was Sameh, had missed her then and she often justified her absence by pretending to go to the rest room to fix her makeup. Sometimes this took such a long time and one day when she was late he followed her; he had never doubted her before. Having already escaped his suspicious wife, he thought that he was safe from doubts in Belly of the Whale with the one he loved. He believed everyone on board were dedicated and respectful and there was no room for betrayal nor doubts on board.

When Mourad came into the kitchen he saw Edward and Shaima kissing. Stunned, he gasped and held back his anger to keep watching them. Somehow the scene had attracted him; he was bored with love-making and the idea of watching love just like he used to do on TV when he was on land made him happy. For a moment, he remembered that Shaima was nothing but an illusion who had no real existence on land; she was a mermaid in Belly of the Whale and that was all. One scene followed the other until the love scenes between Edward and Shaima ended. Mourad, contrary to what was expected from him, clapped his hands happily and encouragingly. His reaction intensely provoked Nouria who soon regained her barbarian nature. In a blink of an eye, she hurried and grabbed the biggest knife and stabbed Mourad mercilessly until he fell dead to the utter amazement of Edward the chef and other guests who had surrounded them to see what had happened.

Nouria rioted like a monster; no one had expected her to explode like a volcano in such a manner. Her madness and terror forced everyone to keep silent and never tell what had happened in front of their eyes. Mourad's reality was discovered by the truth detectors and he was no better than Ma'ally. Dr. Sakina, however, was not deceived; she consulted Dr. Ramzy and wondered about what was really happening. They both agreed to secretly investigate the truth of the matter. Ma'ally's accident was still at the back of Dr. Sakina's mind, irritating her still pulsing conscience. She felt at heart that there was something wrong behind that incident. She had expected the possibility of surprises occurring on board of Belly of the Whale but she could never make sure that Ma'ally's bleeding was due to the pressure of water in the bottom of the sea, or because of the steroids and the drink of life, or whether it could be only due to her fate that Belly of the Whale could not stop. They had ensured them that there was no death or life on board and that life on board was only one non ending party. Dr. Sakina harshly reproached herself: I was stupid and naive to believe in this dirty game; I have to do something; I have to save those who are still on board of this monstrous ship. She decided to speak to Manaz to find out whether she and Edward were really in a relationship. She justified her questions to Manaz by pretending that she was conducting a research about life in Belly of the Whale to find out whether it was a good experience and to correct any mistakes that could have happened. Manaz, incited by jealousy and anger because of Edward's betrayal of her, told Dr. Sakina that Mozafar had stayed with her during the time Dr. Sakina was helping the late Ma'ally. Manaz also confided to Sakina that she had watched the love scene in the kitchen between Edward and Shaima. She had never liked Shaima and when she noticed that she disappeared from the hall and followed her she saw what happened in the kitchen. Mozafar was drunk then and he did not notice that she had left and returned while he was waiting for her in the bar.

Dr. Sakina did not comment on Manaz's words; all she cared about was how to get out of the deadlock that could endanger the lives of nine hundred ninety eight persons on board. It was clear that life in Belly of the Whale started to head towards a dead end; the idea of perpetual orgasm did not work anymore. As for Shaima, Dr. Sakina had a feeling that she was somehow involved in Edward's murder. The false pretext of telling the truth became the only way of committing crimes on board of Belly of the Whale.

Though Dr. Ramzy had a different opinion, he promised Dr. Sakina to help her as far as he could in educating the residents and attempting to awaken them from their deep slumber and in discussing the prospect of ending the trip with them. He believed that nothing was impossible and since they had chosen to come to Belly of the Whale, it was natural that it was up for them to take the decision and go back.

Ramzy's problem was that, as a surgeon, he had spent his whole life in the operation room facing only challenges at the level of his profession. He had succeeded in most of the surgeries despite the hard conditions they involved. He had studied and graduated in the United States of America and continued his study and research in Latin American and Chinese medicine.

Ramzy did not conceal his regret about participating in the no return journey. Though he had been depressed before joining Belly of the Whale, he had a much wider life on land than his life in that vulgar paradise prison. When he decided to join the journey he was in a state of confusion and incomplete awareness. His depression got worse with the discovery of Ma'ally's death; she was his real wife and her original name was San'aa; he had always loved her ever since they got married. Their love story was wasted by betrayals and family disputes that could have been avoided had he thought that she would end up between the jaws of sharks. He did not know back them that he would end up as the rescuer of the souls of people who came to Belly of the Whale with the intention to never return. What if the residents refused to go back? What will happened to all of us if we return? How would we look like? How long have we been away and who will be waiting for us? Have we aged? Or did we die then were resurrected? What happened to us? We will never know the answers as long as we stay her; but I want to go back; I am now sure I want to. This was what Ramzy had decided, even if it meant he would be all by himself. Oh God, how painful it is to see the one you love commit suicide in front of you! That was exactly what happened to Ma'ally? He had found out through the clinical records that Ma'ally had conceived, and that she took the decision to have an abortion, though she was aware of the dangers of her decision. He was sure she was San'aa, since the terms and conditions of the shark game necessitated that the real name of the deceased must be revealed. What if Edward's wife came and asked who he was? What if the real wife knew that the victim Edward was Rozario? His mother was foreign and his father was an Arab and he had suffered from discrimination because of the fair color of his skin and was accused of not belonging to Islam? What if his wife, whoever she was, had the courage to disclose her identity so that her husband Rozario, who had been an example of decency and high conduct throughout his life, could have the funeral that he deserved? Even in Belly of the Whale, in which everyone pretended to be perfect and flawless, she could never find anyone as decent as the late Rozario. But Rozario's unknown wife never appeared and never disclosed her identity. How could she do that when she knew for sure that it would lead to her predetermined end? She must have recognized him, or at least had recognized his body parts being torn by sharks in front of her eyes. Ramzy believed that if she had not recognize him then she had never really known him well all her life.

Ramzy was dominated by curiosity; he hoped to find that lady, the late Edward's wife; he hoped that she might disclose her identity; he hoped that she could be generous and noble and would be convinced that they must leave Belly of the whale! He would go around searching all faces, or rather, all masks on board for a woman like that and maybe he might find some hidden features of a sad lady who had lost her poor husband in Belly of the Whale, even though he had cheated on her.

Ramzy discussed the idea of searching for Edward's wife with Dr. Sakina and she agreed with him that persuading the victim's wife might help to increase the number of those who believed that their departure was necessary. Seeing her husband killed must have affected her emotions and revived some human compassion that was dead, or at least had been narcotized or made numb on that sinister ship. But how could they find her? After discussing different methods to attract the lady they had targeted, Sakina and Ramzy agreed to make use of scientific theories to help them reveal her identity. They decided to use the truth detectors to handle that matter; Dr. Sakina announced that all ladies on board of Belly of the Whale had to undergo an obligatory clinical investigation to make sure they do not suffer from breast cancer which might discreetly endanger their lives.

With the beginning of the clinical investigations, side talks between Sakina and the ladies started. Most of their talks were away from the truth detectors until one lady complained of excruciating stomachache which was probably the result of emotional anguish. Gradually, that lady, Ra'eeda, confessed her sadness over her husband Rozario, not caring about the truth detectors or the death penalty. After watching her husband disappear between the sharks' jaws, she no longer found any meaning or justification for life in that ornamented, merciless tomb of a ship. She believed all people on board were fierce monsters who knew nothing about humanity and certainly did not belong to the human race; they were merely lavishly wealthy people who came to the ship for cheer pleasure and wondered what to be expected from them.

Ra'eeda admitted her regret about participating in that adventure and agreed with Sakina and Ramzy about the need of a plan to convince the rest of the residents of the necessity to leave the ship. But how could they do this with all the eavesdropping devices and truth detectors lurking everywhere; let alone the measuring of the amount of drink consumed by everyone to keep them happy, active, intoxicated and full of life. On Belly of the Whale, life was complete happiness that was how it was supposed to be.

Sakina suggested that they should involve Mozafar in their game since she had lately noticed that he was unhappy and distracted. As his partner, she proposed to persuade him using all sorts of love making tactics, though she herself had no desire for sex anymore despite the pleasure drink she had. Mozafar, she thought, had strong well and big heart and would not disclose their secret.

As director of many companies and fast food chain restaurants, Maher, whose name on Belly of the Whale was Mozafar, had a great deal of acumen and managerial skills. His sharp cinematic memory was still able to function well despite all the energizing drink with its blurring effect on memories. He recalled the face of young Khalid on the day he shouted at the top of his voice announcing to everyone that he was the one in charge of all computers who controlled all devices in Belly of the Whale. Khalid's face, though masked, revealed that he was telling the truth even though he later ridiculously denied all what he had said. The truth detectors could not catch that at the time, or maybe they did but Khalid could delete all evidence against himself if he was really in charge of computers. Maher suggested that they should go ahead and try to convince Khalid anyway since they have nothing to lose; he believed that they were already as good as dead.

They all agreed to make an attempt to gain Khalid to their side despite their fear he might refuse the idea. How would they avoid his evil doings in case he refused? Would he let them save others and suggest the idea that everyone on board should go back. Would he allow everyone on board decide his own destiny? Would he seize the opportunity to tighten his clutch over everything on board? Dr. Ramzy suggested that they should keep Khalid under anesthesia and communicate directly with the residents who had started to wither out and looked exhausted, burned out and unsatisfied.

Sakina, on the other hand, suggested that they should first make sure if Khalid was really the computer administrator through a fake clinical examination during which truth radars should be paused for a period of time. This would enable Dr. Sakina and Dr. Ramzy to ask him direct and indirect questions and give them a chance to read his body language and get some additional information about him.

Ra'eeda offered to help them using her feminine weapons to make Khalid fall in love with her. Based on her own experience, a man in love would tell the most unimaginable secrets to his beloved; nothing would prevent him, not even truth detectors.

After a long discussion they all agreed that Sakina should convince Khalid to undertake a brain cells clinical examination. She would use the pretext that the investigation was necessary to prevent brain damage that might result from severe fatigue and frequent consumption of steroids and water pressure, things which may positively affect the growth of cancer cells.

Convinced, Khalid went to have the examination and during the process Sakina and Ramzy become certain that he was really in charge of computers on board and that there was no way he would ever give up the dream which he had worked hard to achieve. He also expressed his a severe animosity for anyone who would merely think about leaving the ship or changing the prearranged plan.

Both Sakina and Ramzy noticed Khalid's hostility and sensitivity towards taking to others about leaving the ship. He had proven his unmatched desire to control others and that made them more cautious and worried. They knew that he was capable of evil deeds and that he would do whatever it took to prevent them from going back to land. So, they decided to do without him and not to wait for his consent to convince others. They would keep him under control and close observation because sooner or later he would find out their plan, which he believed to be capital treason that deserved death penalty. He would force them to commit suicide according to the vow of The Whale which they had signed before embarking into this horrible game.

Part Twelve, the Finale

B ASED ON THE INFORMATION THEY gathered, the rescue team,
which consisted of Ramzy, Sakina, Ra'eeda and Maher, agreed
to talk to all of the residents of Belly of the Whale individually
according to a plan that would not allow Khalid to find out about
these side conversations. They mainly depended on the medical team
made up of Sakina and Ramzy both of whom exerted mighty efforts
to convince the residents that they have become sick and that they will
die of suffocation or depression or by suicide or even out of ecstasy if
they stayed any longer in Belly of the Whale. They told them that
there was no paradise or eternity on the ship and that its laws of were
contradictory to natural law and that this itself was enough reason
for the failure of the experiment no matter how long it went on. They
assured the residents that regrets would never do them any good and
that it was better to take action quickly and leave the ship alive as soon
as possible since a minute on the ship might equal a whole year on land.

The medical team, however, faced a lot of rejection when they
mentioned the concept of time and many residents expressed their
fears about returning to land. They asked the team frequent questions:
"What would happen to us? How would we look? And what news
would we hear when we go back? What if nobody alive on land could
recognize us? What if our grandchildren had already grown old and
died?

Despite all the sexual advances that Maher and Ra'eeda made
to convince the residents, many of them preferred to keep the status

quo. The rescue team sank deeply into depression and this led them to drink more of the drink of that nefarious drink, as they had come to call it. They continued to dance, or at least pretended to be cheerful and happy.

Lucy and Kamal started to feel that their bodies were waning; they wanted to do nothing but sleep, which they did not do since they came into the journey of eternal delusion. Gradually Basma and Riyad felt the same way; they were extremely depressed and anxious to leave the ship even if it meant they would eventually die. After discussing this, the four of them agreed on a suicide pact, also drawing others in to collectively end their lives in Belly of the Whale, a hopeless response to Khalid's manipulation, his threats of death to anyone who contemplated leaving the ship. The truth detectors were deactivated and this enabled everyone to remove the mask and reveal their true identities. The suicide team did their best to tell others that the detectors were deactivated for their own good. They assured everyone that God would abandon them or punish them in Hell; God would forgive their sins because they have been intoxicated and had lived under unnatural circumstances. Committing suicide was the least they could do to prove their faith and it certainly was better than submitting to the criminal Khalid. Matters on board got worse and many people could not understand the harsh reality of their existence and the betrayals that took place in front of them as if they were in a trance. They suddenly woke up to the shocking huge disaster they found themselves entangled into.

As a result of the sudden amazing changes that the residents underwent both physically and psychologically, they formed several different group. Each group had its own point of view about methods of solving the problem. The creator of the idea of using false names and wearing masks, Fadel, known by the name Jalal, joined the group that wanted to go back safe and sound. Thus, he supported Dr. Fawzy's group, and so did Batla, previously known by the name of Hend, who had influenced him through her romantic ways. Salima, known as Mayada, joined the suicide group. She wished that her servant had killed her because that would have given her the honor to die as a martyr instead of committing suicide for the sake of eternity. She did not have any hope of survival or getting out of Belly of the Whale alive because of the threats of Khalid who had turned into a monster. He was selfishness and possessive or maybe he was committed to seal the deal with some people on land.

Sarya, or the wicked Basma, wife of the barren Mubarak, preferred to join Khalid, who lately called himself Raa'id and who was in charge of the computers and devices on board. Sarya chose him out of love; she did not know the reason she fell in love with him in Belly of the Whale; she did not know if she did because they both had many mutual qualities, or because they were totally different. She decided to announce to everyone that she would not leave the ship unless she was with him.

Beautiful Marwa decided to travel to France with Sam in order to help him achieve his goal by displaying his paintings in Louvre and to abandon the illusion of Belly of the Whale with its sapphire and alabaster. They both agreed to move to Italy so that Sam could make his dream come true by competing with the works of Da Vinci. But decisions were easier taken than carried out and Marwa had nothing to lose since that earthquake demolished her family and threw her as hostage into Belly of the Whale. So she was up to the risk and decided to escape with Sam without asking for permission from anyone.

Marwa's dreams to travel vanish into thin air when a shark clutched her leg as she tried to escape. Trying to save his beloved whom he could not live without, Sam threw himself in front of the shark but at no avail. More blood scattered on the windows of Belly of the Whale in a horrific scene that scared the rest of the residents and made them avoid the least movement to save what was left of their already fading away energy. The drink they had been consuming since the beginning of the journey was slowly poisoning them; they wished it was a fast acting lethal poison so that they could end their perpetual severe and unimaginable torture.

Technology obsessed Khalid, or Raa'id, became hysteric after Dr. Sakina had slyly put the sleeping pills into his drink hoping that he might sleep or die. It was clear she no longer enjoyed the vigilant professional conscience which she used to have and never thought would lose one day. Khalid was the greatest source of danger and getting rid of him was the only solution to let others go out of the ship. But the pills, due to the effect of the pleasure drink, affected Khalid in a hysteric manner. He got mad and with the help of Sarya, he could put the residents into fetters and chains. Sarya did not respond to her poor husband Mubarak's pleas to release him. Provoked by her response, Mubarak unconsciously exposed their private memories during intercourse without the slightest regard for privacy or traditions. He enumerated her pleasure-inciting body parts, the nicknames he loved to call her, the various sex positions they had together whether they had previously planned them or just did spontaneously. Calling her stupid, he admitted that he had cheated on her and that she had never noticed and enumerated the times he betrayed her. Sarya was provoked to the point that she too admitted her lesbian affairs and the men and women she had slept with whom he had never noticed; she called him "barren". That was the word that caught the attention of Doctor Sakina who had believed that Ma'aaly was bearing his own child.

In the midst of this affray and thanks to Allah and with His help, Khalid called for the first time some unknown party whom Sarya did not know, and perhaps never would. According to that party all the nonbelievers on board were gotten rid of; they were the enemies of religion who believed in no God. Some suicide groups were secretly formed that had convinced the nonbelievers with the exception of some anarchists who rejected the decision to commit suicide. They were convinced out of their own suffering to be chained and tossed into the ocean in a process of mass suicide. Those too, were shackled in chains and forcibly tossed into the ocean. It became certain that all of them were devoured by sharks and died. The message was delivered to Khalid in a faint voice that seemed to be coming from the world of the dead or from another planet and this frightened her and caused her to faint. When she regained consciousness, she found Raa'id kissing her in a love scene whose details she knew nothing about. She went crazy and asked the monster accused him of raping her while she was unconscious. She thought she was talking to a fellow human being who resembled her in body and soul only to discover that he was a monster deprived from all feelings. His brain cells were removed and his mind was programmed to murder and act violently and criminally; nothing satisfied him but the taste of blood.

Khalid chained her, naked and distorted, to a wall and severely hit her. She begged him using all her femininity asking him to make love to her even if it were for the last time. She promised that she would then be ready to follow in his righteous conquest and follow him anywhere to the end of the world. Her efforts succeeded as he unchained her but soon enough she disappeared, soaked in her blood as Raa'id, her beloved, shot her and escaped in a boat that was specially prepared. That scene was the last to cling to Sarya's memory before she met her Maker on some date, A.H., or perhaps it was some other date, A.D., or maybe yet it was scripted according to the Mayan calendar.

The hermit Ali Eldeen surrendered willingly to the ocean; he closed his eyes and slept dreaming dreamt about going to Heaven and sleeps. Batla, the painter, surrendered to a beautiful dream full of trees, rivers, singing birds and shining sun. She let her slender body float as lightly as a dove's feather on the water holding her breath as if she were a fish until she found herself on shore. She did not believe her eyes and did not even want to think so she closed her eyes again and slept peacefully. She woke up two days later to find herself stretching on a sand beach like the one she had longed for, the one she left with Ali near their cottage. She had missed Ali so much; she wished he was still alive. She did not see him in Belly of the Whale and did not know how he ended up: was he one of the survivors, or did he drown? Was he devoured by a shark? She did not know. She wondered how she failed to recognize him on board despite their great love. Would he be able to recognize her at that moment? How could not he recognize her among the women on board of that hell, the hateful Whale ship? Batla asked herself: "I wonder how I look! I need to see my face, how old am I now? What happened to me? Where am I now? I have no idea."

Heavenly Will saved Ali in a miraculous manner; he did not even recognize how he had survived. All he remembered was that he had wholeheartedly resorted to Allah for help. He was now in a hospital on the shore to be treated from many bruises and fungal infections and inflammations that had covered his thin body. Doctors, however, failed to specify the liquid that was spotted in his liver and expressed their fear that it was too late for his damaged body to recover and get rid of the remains of that poison which was still hurting his liver.

Feeling death approaching him, Ali Eldeen was perfectly satisfied and content. Meanwhile he took a glimpse to a big screen on the wall that was a bit smaller than a cinema screen and looked more or less like a TV. He listened to what used to be called the news before, and heard an obituary of the residents of Belly of the Whale. It was a death announcement of everyone on board of the ship after losing any hope of finding any survivors. He found out that it was only a year since the delusive journey had started and that it was a conspiracy made by multinational companies to send the elite of thinkers, innovators, financiers and the faithful to a journey of no return in order to rob them out of their property. The number of the deceased had exceeded seven hundred, four hundred of them were men and the rest were women. Their distraught families were then trying to identify the bodies and they refused to talk to the media.

About the Translator

D R. ABEER ELGAMAL IS ASSISTANT professor of English language and literature; she has studied and taught English literature and translation in several universities in Egypt, The United States of America, and the Gulf. Currently she teaches at the Department of Foreign Languages, Mansoura University, Egypt.

She is an author and blogger who writes in Arabic and English and translates books, mostly literature, in the same language pair. Her short stories and blog posts have featured in several publications both printed and electronic. She recently published a book entitled **Mothers on a Tough Mission** in Cairo with Lilith Publishing House and is currently working on the final draft of her English novel **The Scent of Paper** and the translation of a book for the Egyptian National center for Translation. Dr. Abeer is very proud of being a wife and a mother of four wonderful children and she considers her family the main source of her inspiration. You can visit her at http://abeerelgamal.blogspot.com.eg/ or http://momentsfromlife-abeerelgamal.blogspot.com.eg/